I LOVE YOU, BABY SHARK

Doo Doo Doo Doo Doo Doo

Art by John John Bajet

Cartwheel Books
An Imprint of Scholastic Inc.
New York

ISBN 978-1-338-60634-8

10 9 8 7 6 5 4 3   19 20 21 22 23

Printed in the U.S.A.   40
First printing, December 2019
Designed by Doan Buu

Wherever you swim,
be it near or far,
my heart will be with you
wherever you are.
From the light of day,
to the night so dark,
I will always love you,

BABY SHARK!

Hold you tight, doo doo doo doo doo doo.
Hold you tight, doo doo doo doo doo doo.

Day and night, doo doo doo doo doo doo.
Day and night, doo doo doo doo doo doo.

Day and night, doo doo doo doo doo doo.
DAY AND NIGHT!

Give a hug, doo doo doo doo doo doo.
Give a hug, doo doo doo doo doo doo.

Safe and snug, doo doo doo doo doo doo.
Safe and snug, doo doo doo doo doo doo.
Safe and snug, doo doo doo doo doo doo.

SAFE AND SNUG!

Near or far, doo doo doo doo doo doo.
Near or far, doo doo doo doo doo doo doo.

Near or far, doo doo doo doo doo doo. **NEAR OR FAR!**

Shining star, doo doo doo doo doo doo.
Shining star, doo doo doo doo doo doo doo.

Shining star, doo doo doo doo doo doo.
SHINING STAR!

Blow a kiss, doo doo doo doo doo doo.
Blow a kiss, doo doo doo doo doo doo.

Make a wish, doo doo doo doo doo doo.
Make a wish, doo doo doo doo doo doo.

Make a wish, doo doo doo doo doo doo. **MAKE A WISH!**

Head to toe, doo doo doo doo doo doo doo.
Head to toe, doo doo doo doo doo doo doo.

Head to toe, doo doo doo doo doo doo. **HEAD TO TOE!**

Love you so, doo doo doo doo doo.
Love you so, doo doo doo doo doo doo.
Love you so, doo doo doo doo doo doo doo.

LOVE YOU SO!
I LOVE YOU, BABY SHARK!

I LOVE YOU, BABY SHARK DANCE!

HOLD YOU TIGHT!
Cross your arms in front tightly and rock back and forth.

DAY AND NIGHT!
Bring your hands together over your head to make a hand circle.

GIVE A HUG!
Bring your arms together for a hug.

SAFE AND SNUG!
Rock your arms like a cradle.

NEAR OR FAR!
Point here and there.

SHINING STAR!
Starting above your head, wiggle your fingers back and forth like star dust.

BLOW A KISS!
Blow a kiss.

MAKE A WISH!
Move your finger across the sky.

HEAD TO TOE!
Point from your head down to your toes and back.

LOVE YOU SO!
Make heart hands.